MW00790686

Another set of preachers tell their congregations, that God predestinated, and selected from all eternity, a certain number to be saved and a certain number to be damned eternally. If this were true, *the day of judgment* IS PAST: *their preaching* is in vain, and they had better work at some useful calling for their livelihood.

This doctrine, also like the former, hath a direct tendency to demoralize mankind. Can a bad man be reformed by telling him, that if he is one of those who was decreed to be damned before he was born, his reformation will do him no good ; and if he was decreed to be saved, he will be saved, whether he believes it or not ; for this is the result of the doctrine. Such preaching and such preachers do injury to the moral world. They had better be at the plough.

As, in my political works, my motive and object have been to give man an elevated sense of his own character, and free him from the slavish and superstitious absurdity of monarchy and hereditary government, so, in my publications on religious subjects, my endeavours have been directed to bring man to a right use of the reason that God has given him ; to impress on him the great principles of divine morality, justice, and mercy, and a benevolent disposition to all men, and to all creatures, and to inspire in him a spirit of trust, confidence and consolation, in his Creator, unshackled by the fables of books pretending to be *the word of God.*

THOMAS PAINE.

INTRODUCTION.

As a great deal is said in the New Testament about Dreams, it is first necessary to explain the nature of dreams, and to shew by what operation of the mind a dream is produced during sleep. When this is understood, we shall be the better enabled to judge whether any reliance can be placed upon them; and consequently, whether the several matters in the New Testament related of dreams deserve the credit which the writers of that book and priests and commentators ascribe to them.

AN

ESSAY ON DREAMS,

&c.

IN order to understand the nature of dreams, or of that which passes in ideal vision during a state of sleep, it is first necessary to understand the composition and decomposition of the human mind.

The three great faculties of the mind are IMAGINATION, JUDGMENT, and MEMORY. Every action of the mind comes under one or other of these faculties. In a state of wake-fulness, as in the day-time, these three faculties are all active; but that is seldom the case in sleep, and never per-fectly; and this is the cause that our dreams are not so regular and rational as our waking thoughts.

The seat of that collection of powers or faculties, that constitute what is called the mind, is in the brain. There is not, and cannot be, any visible demonstration of this anatomically, but accidents, happening to living persons, shew it to be so. An injury done to the brain, by a fracture of the skull, will sometimes change a wise man into a child-ish idiot; a being without mind. But so careful has nature been of that *sanctum sanctorum* of man, the brain, that of all the external accidents to which humanity is subject, this happens the most seldom. But we often see it happening by long habitual intemperance.

Whether those three faculties occupy distinct apartments of the brain, is known only to that Almighty power that formed and organized it. We can see the external effects of muscular motion in all the members of the body, though its *primum mobile*, or first moving cause, is unknown to man. Our external motions are sometimes the effect of intention, and sometimes not. If we are sitting and intend to rise, or standing and intend to sit, or to walk, the limbs obey that intention as if they heard the order given. But we make a thousand motions every day, and those waking as well as sleeping, that have no prior intention to direct them. Each member acts as if it had a will or mind of its own. Man governs the whole, when he pleases to govern, but, in the

interims, the several parts, like little suburbs, govern themselves, without consulting the sovereign.

All these motions, whatever be the generatiug cause,
are external and visible. But with respect to the brain, no
ocular observation can be made upon it. All is mystery;
all is darkness in that womb of thought.

Whether the brain be a mass of matter in continual rest;
whether it has a vibrating pulsative motion, or a heaving
and falling motion, like matter in fermentation; whether
different parts of the brain have different motions according
to the faculty that is employed, be it the imagination, the
judgment, or the memory, man knows not He knows
not the cause of his own wit. His own brain conceals
it from him.

Comparing invisible by visible things, as metaphysical
can sometimes be compared to physical things, the operations
of these distinct and several faculties have some resemblance
to the mechanism of a watch. The main spring, which puts
all in motion, corresponds to the imagination; the pendulum
or balance, which corrects and regulates that motion, corresponds to the judgment; and the hand and dial, like the
memory, record the operations.

In proportion as these several faculties sleep, slumber,
or keep awake, during the continuance of a dream, in
that proportion the dream will be reasonable or frantic,
remembered or forgotten.

If there is any faculty in mental man that never sleeps,
it is that volatile thing the imagination; the case is different
with the judgment and memory. The sedate and sober
constitution of the judgment easily disposes it to rest; and
as to the memory, it records in silence, and is active only
when it is called upon.

That the judgment soon goes to sleep may be perceived
by our sometimes beginning to dream before we are fully
asleep ourselves. Some random thought runs in the mind,
and we start, as it were, into recollection, that we are
dreaming between sleeping and waking.

If the judgment sleeps, whilst the imagination keeps awake,
the dream will be a riotous assemblage of mis-shapen images and ranting ideas, and the more active the imagination
is, the wilder the dream will be. The most inconsistent
and the most impossible things will appear right; because
that faculty, whose province it is to keep order, is in a state
of absence. The master of the school is gone out, and the
boys are in an uproar.

If the memory sleeps, we shall have no other knowledge of the dream than that we have dreamt, without knowing what it was about. In this case, it is sensation, rather than recollection, that acts. The dream has given us some sense of pain or trouble, and we feel it as a hurt, rather than remember it as a vision.

If memory only slumbers, we shall have a faint remembrance of the dream, and, after a few minutes, it will sometimes happen, that the principal passages of the dream will occur to us more fully. The cause of this is, that the memory will sometimes continue slumbering or sleeping after we are awake ourselves, and that so fully, that it may, and sometimes does, happen, that we do not immediately recollect where we are, nor what we have been about, or have to do. But when the memory starts into wakefulness, it brings the knowledge of these things back upon us, like a flood of light, and sometimes the dream with it.

But the most curious circumstance of the mind, in a state of dream, is the power it has to become the agent of every person, character and thing, of which it dreams. It carries on conversation with several, asks questions, hears answers, gives and receives information, and it acts all these parts itself.

But however various and eccentric the imagination may be in the creation of images and ideas, it cannot supply the place of memory, with respect to things that are forgotten when we are awake. For example, if we have forgotten the name of a person, and dream of seeing him, of asking him his name, he cannot tell it; for it is ourselves asking ourselves the question.

But though the imagination cannot supply the place of real memory, it has the wild faculty of counterfeiting memory. It dreams of persons it never knew, and talks with them as if it had remembered them as old acquaintances. It relates circumstances that never happened, and tells them as if they had happened. It goes to places that never existed, and knows where all the streets and houses are as if it had been there before. The scenes it creates often appear as scenes remembered. It will sometimes act a dream within a dream, and, in the delusion of dreaming, tell a dream it never dreamed, and tell it as if it was from memory. It may also be remarked, that the imagination, in a dream, has no idea of time, *as time*. It counts only by circumstances; and if a succession of circumstances pass in a dream that would require a great length of time to accomplish them,

It will appear to the dreamer that a length of time equal thereto has passed also.

As this is the state of the mind in dreams, it may rationally be said, that every person is mad once in twenty-four hours, for were he to act in the day as he dreams in the night, he would be confined for a lunatic. In a state of wakefulness, those three faculties being all active, and acting in union constitute the rational man. In dreams, it is otherwise, and therefore that state which is called insanity appears to be no other than a disunion of those faculties and a cessation of the judgment, during wakefulness, that we so often experience during sleep; and idiotcy, into which some persons have fallen, is that cessation of all the faculties, of which we can be sensible, when we happen to wake before our memory.

In this view of the mind, how absurd is it to place reliance upon dreams, and how much more absurd to make them a foundation for religion; yet the belief that Jesus Christ is the Son of God, begotten by the Holy Ghost, a being never heard of before, stands on the story of an old man's dream. " *And behold the angel of the Lord appeared to Joseph in a dream, saying, Joseph, thou son of David, fear not thou to take unto thee Mary thy wife, for that which is conceived in her is of the Holy Ghost.*"—Matt. ch. i. v. 20.

After this we have the childish stories of three or four other dreams; about Joseph going into Egypt; about his coming back again; about this, and about that; and this story of dreams has thrown Europe into a dream for more than a thousand years. All the efforts that nature, reason, and conscience have made to awaken man from it, have been ascribed by priestcraft and superstition to the workings of the devil, and had it not been for the American revolution, which by establishing the *universal right of conscience* first opened the way to free discussion, and for the French revolution which followed, this religion of dreams had continued to be preached, and that after it had ceased to be believed. Those who preached it and did not believe it, still believed the delusion necessary. They were not bold enough to be honest, nor honest enough to be bold.

Every new religion, like a new play, requires a new apparatus of dresses and machinery, to fit the new characters it creates. The story of Christ in the New Testament brings a new being upon the stage, which it calls the Holy Ghost; and the story of Abraham, the father of the Jews, in the Old Testament, gives existence to a new order of beings it calls Angels—There was no Holy Ghost before the time of Christ,

nor Angels before the time of Abraham.—We hear nothing
of these winged gentlemen, till more than two thousand
years, according to the Bible chronology, from the time they
say the heavens, the earth, and all therein were made:—
After this, they hop about as thick as birds in a grove:—The
first we hear of, pays his addresses to Hagar in the wilderness; then three of them visit Sarah; another wrestles a fall
with Jacob; and these birds of passage, having found their
way to earth and back, are continually coming and going.—
They eat and drink, and up again to heaven.—What they
do with the food, they carry away in their bellies, the Bible
does not tell us.—Perhaps they do as the birds do, discharge
it as they fly, for neither the scripture nor the church hath
told us there are necessary houses for them in heaven.

One would think that a system, loaded with such gross and
vulgar absurdities as scripture religion is, could never have
obtained credit; yet we have seen what priestcraft and
fanaticism could do, and credulity believe.

From angels in the Old Testament, we get to prophets, to
witches, to seers of visions, and dreamers of dreams, and
sometimes we are told, as in 2 Sam. chap. ix. ver. 15, that
God whispers in the ear—At other times, we are not told
how the impulse was given, or whether sleeping or waking—
In 2 Sam. chap. xxiv. ver. 1, it is said, " *And again the an-
ger of the Lord was kindled against Israel, and he moved
David against them to say go number Israel and Judah.*"—
And in 1 Chron, chap. xxi. ver. 1, when the same story is
again related, it is said, " *and Satan stood up against
Israel, and moved David to number Israel.*"

Whether this was done sleeping or waking, we are not
told, but it seems that David, whom they call " a man after
God's own heart," did not know by what spirit he was moved; and as to the men called inspired penmen, they agree so
well about the matter, that, in one book, they say that it
was God, and in the other, that it was the Devil.

Yet this is the trash that the church imposes upon the
world as the word of God; this is the collection of lies and
contradictions, called the Holy Bible! this is the rubbish
called revealed religion!

The idea that writers of the Old Testament had of a God
was boisterous, contemptible and vulgar.—They make him
the Mars of the Jews, the fighting God of Israel, the conjuring God of their Priests and Prophets.—They tell as
many fables of him as the Greeks told of Hercules.

They pit him against Pharaoh, as it were to box with him,
and Moses carries the challenge; they make their God to

say, insultingly, " *I will get me honour upon Pharaoh, and upon his Host, upon his Chariots and upon his Horsemen.*"—And that he may keep his word, they make him set a trap in the Red Sea, in the dead of the night, for Pharaoh, his host, and his horses, and drown them as a rat-catcher would so many rats—Great honour indeed! the story of Jack the Giant-killer is better told!

They match him against the Egyptian magicians, to conjure with him, and after bad conjuring on both sides, (for where there is no great contest, there is no great honour) they bring him off victorious; the three first essays are a dead match—Each party turns his rod into a serpent, the rivers into blood, and creates frogs; but upon the fourth, the God of the Israelites obtains the laurel, he covers them all over with lice!—The Egyptian magicians cannot do the same, and this lousy triumph proclaims the victory!

They make their God to rain fire and brimstone upon Sodom and Gomorrah, and belch fire and smoke upon mount Sinai; as if he was the Pluto of the lower regions.—They make him salt up Lot's wife like pickled pork; they make him pass like Shakspeare's Queen Mab into the brain of their priests, prophets, and prophetesses, and tickle them into dreams, and after making him play all kind of tricks, they confound him with Satan, and leave us at a loss to know what God they meant!

This is the descriptive God of the Old Testament; and as to the New, though the authors of it have varied the scene, they have continued the vulgarity.

Is man ever to be the dupe of priestcraft, the slave of superstition? Is he never to have just ideas of his Creator? It is better not to believe there is a God, than to believe of him falsely. When we behold the mighty universe that surrounds us, and dart our contemplation into the eternity of space, filled with innumerable orbs, revolving in eternal harmony, how paltry must the tales of the Old and New Testaments, prophanely called the word of God, appear to thoughtful man! The stupendous wisdom, and unerring order, that reign and govern throughout this wonderous whole, and call us to reflection, *put to shame the Bible!*——The God of eternity and of all that is real, is not the God of passing dreams, and shadows of man's imagination! The God of truth is not the God of fable; the belief, of a God begotten and a God crucified, is a God blasphemed.——It is making a profane use of reason.

I shall conclude this Essay on Dreams with the two first

verses of the 34th chapter of Ecclesiasticus, one of the books of the Apocrypha.

V. i. " *The hopes of a man void of understanding are vain and false; and dreams lift up fools—Whoso regardeth dreams is like him that catcheth at a shadow, and followeth after the wind.*"

I now proceed to an examination of the passages in the Bible called prophecies of the coming of Christ, and to shew there are no prophecies of any such person. That the passages clandestinely styled prophecies are not prophecies, and that they refer to circumstances the Jewish nation was in at the time they were written or spoken, and not to any distance of future time or person.

AN EXAMINATION

OF THE

PASSAGES IN THE NEW TESTAMENT,

Quoted from the Old, and called Prophecies of the coming of Jesus Chrst.

The passages, called Prophecies of or concerning Jesus Christ in the Old Testament, may be classed under the two following heads :—

First, those referred to in the four books of the New Testament, called the four Evangelists, *Matthew, Mark, Luke,* and *John.*

Secondly, those which translators and commentators have, of their own imagination, erected into prophecies, and dubbed with that title at the head of the several chapters of the Old Testament. On these, it is scarcely worth while to waste time, ink, and paper upon; I shall, therefore, confine myself chiefly to those referred to in the aforesaid four books of the New Testament. If I shew that these are not prophecies of the person called Jesus Christ, nor have referance to any such person, it will be perfectly needless to combat those which translators or the Church have invented, and for which they had no other authority than their own imagination.

I begin with the book called the Gospel according to St. Matthew.

In the first chap. ver. 18, it is said, " *Now the birth of Jesus Christ was in this wise; when his mother Mary was espoused to Joseph, before they came together,* SHE WAS FOUND WITH CHILD BY THE HOLY GHOST."—This is going a little too fast; because, to make this verse agree with the next, it should have said no more than that *she was found with child:* for the next verse says, " *Then Joseph her husband being a just man, and not willing to make her a public example, was minded to put her away privily.*"—Consequently, Joseph had found out no more than that she was with child, and he knew it was not by himself.

V. 20. " *And while he thought of these things* (that is, whether he should put her away privily, or make a public example of her) *behold the Angel of the Lord appeared to him* IN A DREAM (that is, *Joseph dreamed* that an angel appeared unto him) *saying, Joseph, thou son of David, fear not to take unto thee Mary thy wife, for that which is conceived in her is of the Holy Ghost. And she shall bring forth a son and call his name Jesus: for he shall save his people from their sins.*"

Now, without entering into any discussion upon the merits or demerits of the account here given, it is proper to observe, that it has no higher authority than that of a dream; for it is impossible for a man to behold any thing in a dream but that which he dreams of. I ask not, therefore, whether Joseph (if there was such a man) had such a dream or not; because, admitting he had, it proves nothing. So wonderful and irrational is the faculty of the mind in dreams, that it acts the part of all the characters its imagination creates, and what it thinks it hears from any of them, is no other than what the roving rapidity of its own imagination invents. It is therefore nothing to me what Joseph dreamed of; whether of the fidelity or infidelity of his wife.—I pay no regard to my own dreams, and I should be weak indeed to put faith in the dreams of another.

The verses, that follow those I have quoted, are the words of the writer of the book of Matthew. " *Now* (says he) *all this* (that is all this dreaming and this pregnancy) *was done, that it might be fulfilled which was spoken of the Lord by the Prophet, saying,*

" *Behold a Virgin shall be with child, and shall bring forth a son, and they shall call his name Emmanuel, which, being interpreted, is God with us.*"

This passage is in Isaiah, chap. vii. ver. 14, and the writer of the book of Matthew endeavours to make his readers believe, that this passage is a prophecy of the person called Jesus Christ. It is no such thing—and I go to shew it is not. But it is first necessary, that I explain the occasion of these words being spoken by Isaiah: the reader will then easily perceive, that so far from their being a prophecy of Jesus Christ, they have not the least reference to such a person, or to any thing that could happen in the time that Christ is said to have lived—which was about seven hundred years after the time of Isaiah. The case is this:

On the death of Solomon, the Jewish nation split into two monarchies; one called the kingdom of Judah, the capital of which was Jerusalem ; the other the kingdom of Israel, the capital of which was Samaria. The kingdom of Judah followed the line of David, and the kingdom of Israel that of Saul ; and these two rival monarchies frequently carried on fierce wars against each other.

At the time Ahaz was king of Judah, which was in the time of Isaiah, Pekah was king of Israel: and Pekah joined himself to Rezin, king of Syria, to make war against Ahaz, king of Judah : and these two kings marched a confederated and powerful army against Jerusalem. Ahaz and his people became alarmed at the danger, and " *their hearts were moved as the trees of the wood are moved with the wind.*" Isaiah, chap. vii. ver. 3.

In this perilous situation of things, Isaiah addresses himself to Ahaz, and assures him, in the name of the Lord (the cant phrase of all the prophets), that these two kings should not succeed against him ; and to assure him that this should be the case (the case was however directly contrary *), tells Ahaz to ask a sign of the Lord. This, Ahaz declined doing, giving as a reason, that he would not tempt the Lord ; upon which Isaiah, who pretends to be sent from God, says, v. 14, " Therefore the Lord himself shall give you a sign, *behold, a virgin shall conceive and bear a son*—Butter and honey shall he eat, that he may know to refuse the evil and chuse the

---

* Chron. Chap. xxviii. ver. 1st. *Ahaz was twenty years old when he began to reign, and he reigned sixteen years in Jerusalem, but he did not that which was right in the sight of the Lord—v. 5. Wherefore the Lord his God delivered him into the hand of the king of Syria, and they smote him, and carried away a great multitude of them captive and brought them to Damascus : and he was also delivered into the hand of the king of Israel, who smote him with a great slaughter.*

Ver. 6. *And Pekah (king of Israel) slew in Judah a hundred and twenty thousand in one day ;—v. 8. And the children of Israel carried away captive of their brethren two hundred thousand women, sons, and daughters.*

good—For before the child shall know to refuse the evil and chuse the good, the land, which thou abhorrest, shall be forsaken of both her kings,"—meaning the king of Israel and the king of Syria, who were marching against him.

Here then is the sign, which was to be the birth of a child, and that child a son; and here also is the time limited for the accomplishment of the sign, namely, before the child should know to refuse the evil and chuse the good.

The thing, therefore, to be a sign of success to Ahaz, must be something that would take place before the event of the battle then pending between him and the two kings could be known. A thing to be a sign must precede the thing signified. The sign of rain must be before the rain.

It would have been mockery and insulting nonsense, for Isaiah to have assured Ahaz as a sign, that these two kings should not prevail against him; that a child should be born seven hundred years after he was dead; and that before the child so born should know to refuse the evil and chuse the good, he, Ahaz should be delivered from the danger he was then immediately threatened with.

But the case is, that the child of which Isaiah speaks was his own child, with which his wife or his mistress was then pregnant; for he says in the next chapter, v. 2, " *And I took unto me faithful witnesses to record, Uriah the priest, and Zechariah the son of Jeberechiah ; and I went unto the prophetess, and she conceived and bare a son* ; and he says at v. 18, *of the same chapter,* " *Behold, I and the children whom the Lord hath given me are for signs and for wonders in Israel.*"

It may not be improper here to observe, that the word translated a virgin in Isaiah, does not signify a virgin in Hebrew, but merely a young woman. The tense also is falsified in the translation. Levi gives the Hebrew text of the 14th ver. of the 7th chap. of Isaiah, and the translation in English with it—" *Behold a young woman is with child and beareth a son.*" The expression, says he, is in the present tense. This translation agrees with the other circumstances related of the birth of this child, which was to be a sign to Ahaz. But as the true translation could not have been imposed upon the world as a prophecy of a child to be born seven hundred years afterwards, the Christian translators have falsified the original ; and instead of making Isaiah to say, behold a *young woman* is with child and *beareth* a son ; they make him to say, behold a *virgin shall* conceive and bear a son. It is however only necessary for a person to read the 7th and 8th chapters of Isaiah, and he will be convinced that the passage in question is no prophecy of the person called Jesus Christ. I pass on to the second passage quoted from the Old Testament by the New, as a prophecy of Jesus Christ.

Matthew. chap. ii. ver. 1. "Now when Jesus was born in " Bethlehem of Judah, in the days of Herod the king, behold " there came wise men from the east to Jerusalem— saying, " where is he that is born king of the Jews ? for we have " seen his star in the east, and are come to worship him. " When Herod, the king, heard these things he was trou- "bled, and all Jerusalem with him—and when he had gath- " ered all the chief priests and scribes of the people to- " gether, he demanded of them where Christ should be born "—and they said unto him, in Bethlehem, in the land of " Judea; for thus it is written by the prophet—*and thou* " *Bethlehem, in the land of Judea, art not the least among* " *the Princes of Judea, for out of thee shall come a Governor* " *that shall rule my people Israel*." This passage is in Micah, chap. v. ver. 2.

I pass over the absurdity of seeing and following a star in the day-time, as a man would a *Will with the wisp*, or a candle and lanthorn at night ; and also that of seeing it in the east, when themselves came from the east; for could such a thing be seen at all to serve them for a guide, it must be in the west to them. I confine myself solely to the passage called a prophecy of Jesus Christ.

The book of Micah, in the passage above quoted, chap. v. ver. 2, is speaking of some person, without mentioning his name, from whom some great achievements were expected ; but the description he gives of this person at the 5th ver. proves evidently that it is not Jesus Christ, for he says at the fifth verse, " And *this man* shall be the peace when " the Assyrian shall come into our land, and when he shall "tread in our palaces, then shall we raise up against him " (that is, against the Assyrian) seven shepherds and eight " principal men.—v. 6. And they shall waste the land of " Assyria with the sword, and the land of Nimrod on the "entrance thereof ; thus shall *He* (the person spoken of " at the head of the second verse) deliver us from the Assy- " rian when he cometh into our land, and when he treadeth " within our borders."

This is so evidently descriptive of a military chief, that it cannot be applied to Christ without outraging the character they pretend to give us of him. Besides which, the circumstances of the times here spoken of, and those of the times in which Christ is said to have lived, are in contradiction to

2

each other. It was the Romans, and not the Assyrians, that
had conquered and *were in the land* of Judea, and *trod in
their palaces* when Christ was born, and when he died, and so
far from his driving them out, it was they who signed the war-
rant for his execution, and he suffered under it.

Having thus shewn that this is no prophecy of Jesus Christ,
I pass on to the third passage quoted from the Old Testament
by the new, as a prophecy of him.

This like the first I have spoken of, is introduced by a dream.
Joseph dreameth another dream, and dreameth that he seeth
another angel. The account begins at the 13th v. of 2d chap
of Matthew.

"The angel of the Lord appeared to Joseph in a dream,
"saying, Arise and take the young child and his mother and
"flee into Egypt. and be thou there until I bring thee word :
"For Herod will seek the life of the young child to destroy
"him.—When he arose he took the young child and his
"mother by night and departed into Egypt—and was there
"until the death of Herod, that it might be fulfilled which
"was spoken of the Lord by the prophet, saying *Out of
"Egypt have I called my son.*"

This passage is in the book of Hosea, chap. xi. ver. 1.
The words are, "When Israel was a child then I loved him
"and *called my son out of Egypt*—As they called them, so
"they went from them, they sacrificed unto Baalam and
"burnt incense to graven images.."

This passage, falsely called a prophecy of Christ, refers to
the children of Israel coming out of Egypt in the time of
Pharaoh, and to the idolatry they committed afterwards.
To make it apply to Jesus Christ, he then must be the person
who *sacrificed unto Baalam and burnt incense to graven
images,* for the person called out of Egypt by the collective
name Israel, and the persons committing this idolatry, are the
same persons, or the descendants of them. This then can be
no prophecy of Jesus Christ, unless they are willing to make
an idolator of him. I pass on to the fourth passage called a
prophecy by the writer of the book of Matthew.

This is introduced by a story, told by nobody but himself
and scarcely believed by any body, of the slaughter of all
the children under two years old, by the command of Herod.
A thing which it is not probable could be done by Herod,
as he only held an office under the Roman government, to
which appeals could always be had, as we see in the case
of Paul.

Matthew, however, having made or told his story, says
chap. ii. ver. 17.—"Then was fulfilled that which was

" spoken by Jeremy, the prophet, saying,—*In Ramah was*
" *there a voice heard, lamentation, and weeping and great*
" *mourning: Rachel weeping for her children, and would*
" *not be comforted because they were not.*"

This passage is in Jeremiah, chap. xxxi. ver. 15, and this
verse, when separated from the verses before and after it,
and which explains its application, might with equal propriety be applied to every case of wars, sieges, and other
violences, such as the Christians themselves have often done
to the Jews, where mothers have lamented the loss of their
children. There is nothing in the verse taken singly that
designates or points out any particular application of it,
otherwise than that it points to some circumstance which
at the time of writing it, had already happened, and not to
a thing yet to happen, for the verse is in the preter or past
tense.—I go to explain the case, and shew the application of
the verse.

Jeremiah lived in the time that Nebuchadnezzar besieged,
took, plundered, and destroyed Jerusalem, and led the Jews
captive to Babylon. He carried his violence against the Jews
to every extreme. He slew the sons of king Zedekiah before
his face, he then put out the eyes of Zedekiah, and kept him
in prison till the day of his death.

It is of this time of sorrow and suffering to the Jews that
Jeremiah is speaking. Their temple was destroyed, their
land desolated, their nation and government entirely broken
up, and themselves, men, women, and children, carried into
captivity. They had too many sorrows of their own, immediately before their eyes, to permit them, or any of their
chiefs, to be employing themselves on things that might, or
might not, happen in the world seven hundred years afterwards.

It is, as already observed, of this time of sorrow and suffering to the Jews that Jeremiah is speaking in the verse in
question. In the two next verses, the 16th and 17th, he endeavours to console the sufferers by giving them hopes, and
according to the fashion of speaking in those days, assuran-
ces from the Lord, that their sufferings should have an end,
and that *their children should return again to their own land.*
But I leave the verses to speak for themselves, and the Old
Testament to testify against the New.

Jeremiah, chap. xxxi. ver. 15.—"Thus saith the Lord,
a voice *was* heard in Ramah (it is in the preter tense) lamentation and bitter weeping; Rachel weeping for her children, refused to be comforted for her children because they
were not."

Verse 16.—" Thus saith the Lord, refrain thy voice from
weeping and thine eyes from tears ; for thy work shall be
rewarded, saith the Lord, *and they shall come again from
the land of the enemy.*

Verse 17.—" And there is hope in thine end, saith the
Lord, that *thy children shall come again to their own border.*

By what strange ignorance or imposition is it, that the
children of which Jeremiah speaks (meaning the people of
the Jewish nation, scripturally called *children of Israel,* and
not mere infants under two years old), and who were to return again from the land of the enemy, and come again into
their own borders, can mean the children that Matthew
makes Herod to slaughter? Could those return again from
the land of the enemy, or how can the land of the enemy be
applied to them? Could they come again to their own borders? Good Heavens! How has the world been imposed
upon by Testament makers, priestcraft, and pretended prophecies. I pass on to the fifth passage called a prophecy of
Jesus Christ.

This, like two of the former, is introduced by a dream.
Joseph dreamed another dream, and dreameth of another
Angel. And Matthew is again the historian of the dream
and the dreamer. If it were asked how Matthew could
know what Joseph dreamed, neither the Bishop nor all the
Church could answer the question. Perhaps it was Matthew that dreamed and not Joseph ; that is, Joseph dreamed
by proxy, in Matthew's brain, as they tell us Daniel dreamed
for Nebuchadnezzar. But be this as it may, I go on with
my subject.

The account of this dream is in Matthew, chap. ii. ver. 19.
" But when Herod was dead, behold an angel of the Lord
" appeared in a dream to Joseph in Egypt—Saying, arise
" and take the young child and its mother and go into the
" land of Israel, for they are dead which sought the young
" child's life—and he arose and took the young child and
" his mother and came into the land of Israel. But when
" he heard that Archelaus did reign in Judea in the room
" of his father Herod, he was afraid to go thither. Not-
" withstanding being warned of God in a *dream* (here is
" another dream) he turned aside into the parts of Galilee ;
" and he came and dwelt in a city called *Nazareth, that it
" might be fulfilled which was spoken by the prophets.—He
" shall be called a Nazarene.*"

Here is good circumstantial evidence, that Matthew dreamed, for there is no such passage in all the Old Testament ;
and I invite the bishops and all the priests in Christendom,

including those of America, to produce it.   I pass on to the
sixth passage, called a prophecy of Jesus Christ.

This, as Swift says on another occasion, *is lugged in head*
and shoulders: it needs only to be seen in order to be hooted
as a forced and far-fetched piece of imposition.

Matthew, chap. iv, v. 12.   "Now when Jesus heard that
" John was cast into prison, he departed into Galilee—and
" leaving Nazareth, he came and dwelt in Capernaum, which
" is upon the sea coast, in the borders of Zebulon and Neph-
" thalim—That it might be fulfilled which was spoken by
" Esaias (Isaiah) the prophet, saying, *The land of Zebulon*
" *and the land of Nephthalim, by the way of the sea, beyond*
" *Jordan, in Galilee of the Gentiles—the people which sat in*
" *darkness saw great light, and to them which sat in the re-*
" *gion and shadow of death, light is springing upon them.*"

I wonder Matthew has not made the cris-cross-row, or the
christ-cross-row (I know not how the priests spell it) into
a prophecy.   He might as well have done this as cut out
these unconnected and undescriptive sentences from the place
they stand in, and dubbed them with that title.

The words, however, are in Isaiah, chap. ix. ver. 1, 2, as
follows:—

"Nevertoeless the dimness shall not be such as was in her
vexation, when at the first he lightly afflicted *the land of Ze-*
bulon and the land of Napthali, and afterwards did more
grievously afflict her by the way of the sea, beyond Jordan,
in Galilee of the nations."

All this relates to two circumstances that had already
happened, at the time these words in Isaiah were written.
The one, where the land of Zebulon and Naphthali had been
lightly afflicted, and afterwards more grievously by the way
of the sea.

But observe, reader, how Matthew has falsified the text.
He begins his quotation at a part of the verse where there is
not so much as a comma, and thereby cuts off every thing
that relates to the first affliction.   He then leaves out all that
relates to the second affliction, and by this means leaves out
every thing that makes the verse intelligible, and reduces it
to a senseless skeleton of names of towns.

To bring this imposition of Matthew clearly and imme
diately before the eye of the reader, I will repeat the verse,
and put between crotchets [] the words he has left out, and
put in *Italics* those he has preserved.

[Nevertheless the dimness shall not be such as was in her
vexation when at the first he lightly afflicted] *the land of*

Zebulon and the land of Naphthali. [and did afterwads more grievously afflict her] "by the way of the sea beyond Jordan, in Galilee of the nations.

What gross imposition is it to gut, as the phrase is, a verse in this manner, render it perfectly senseless, and then puff it off on a credulous world as a prophecy.   I proceed to the next verse.

Ver. 2. " The people that walked in darkness have seen a great light : they that dwell in the land of the shadow of death, upon them hath the light shined."   All this is historical, and not in the least prophetical.   The whole is in the preter tense ; it speaks of things that had been accomplished at the time the words were written, and not of things to be accomplished afterwards.

As then the passage is in no possible sense prophetical, nor intended to be so, and that to attempt to make it so, is not only to falsify the original, but to commit a criminal imposition ; it is matter of no concern to us, otherwise than as curiosity, to know who the people were of which the passage speaks, that sat in darkness, and what the light was that had shined in upon them.

If we look into the preceding chapter, the 8th, of which the 9th is only a continuation, we shall find the writer speaking at the 19th verse, of "witches and wizards who peep about and mutter," and of people who made application to them ; and he preaches and exhorts them against this darksome practice.   It is of this people, and of this darksome practice or "walking in darkness," that he is speaking at the 2d verse of the 9th chapter ; and with respect to "the light that had shined in upon them," it refers entirely to his own ministry, and to the boldness of it, which opposed itself to that of "the witches and wizards who peeped about and muttered."

Isaiah is, upon the whole, a wild disorderly writer, preserving in general no clear chain of perception in the arrangement of his ideas, and consequently producing no defined conclusions from them.   It is the wildness of his style, the confusion of his ideas, and the ranting metaphors he employs, that have afforded so many opportunities to priestcraft in some cases, and to superstition in others, to impose those defects upon the world as prophecies of Jesus Christ. Finding no direct meaning in them, and not knowing what to make of them, and supposing at the same time they were intended to have a meaning, they supplied the defect by inventing a meaning of their own, and called it his.   I have, however, in this place, done Isaiah the justice to rescue him from the claws of Matthew, who has torn him unmercifully to pieces ; and from the imposition or ignorance of priests and commentators, by letting Isaiah speak for himself.

If the words *walking in darkness*, and *light breaking in*, could in any case be applied prophetically, which they cannot be, they would better apply to the times we now live in than to any other. The world has " *walked in darkness*" for eighteen hundred years, both as to religion and government, and it is only since the American Revolution began that light has broken in. The belief of *one God*, whose attributes are revealed to us in the book or scripture of the creation, which no human hand can counterfeit or falsify, and not in the written or printed book which, as Matthew has shewn, can be altered or falsified by ignorance or design, is now making its way among us: and as to government, *the light has already gone forth*, and whilst men ought to be careful not to be blinded by the excess of it, as at a certain time in France, when every thing was Robespierean violence, they ought to reverence, and even to adore it, with all the firmness and perseverance that true wisdom can inspire.

I pass on to the seventh passage, called a prophecy of Jesus Christ.

Matthew, chap. viii. ver. 16. " When the evening was come, they brought unto him (Jesus) many that were possessed with devils, and he cast out the spirit with his word, and healed all that were sick.—That it might be fulfilled which was spoken by Esaias (Isaiah) the prophet, saying, " *himself took our infirmities, and bear our sickness.*"

This affair of people being possessed by devils, and of casting them out, was the fable of the day when the books of the New Testament were written. It had not existence at any other time. The books of the Old Testament mention no such thing; the people of the present day know of no such thing; nor does the history of any people or country speak of such a thing. It starts upon us all at once in the book of Matthew, and is altogether an invention of the New Testament-makers and the Christian church. The book of Matthew is the first book where the word *Devil* is mentioned.* We read in some of the books of the Old Testament of things called familiar spirits, the supposed companions of people called witches and wizards. It was no other than the trick of pretended conjurors to obtain money from credulous and ignorant people, or the fabricated charge

---

* The word *devil* is a personification of the word *evil*.

of superstitious malignancy against unfortunate and decre‑ pid old age.

But the idea of a familiar spirit, if we can affix any idea to the term, is exceedingly different to that of being posses‑ sed by a devil. In the one case, the supposed familiar spirit is a dexterous agent, that comes and goes and does as he is bidden: in the other, he is a turbulent roaring monster, that tears and tortures the body into convulsions. Reader, whoever thou art, put thy trust in thy Creator, make use of the reason he endowed thee with, and cast from thee all such fables.

The passage alluded to by Matthew, for as a quotation it is false, is in Isaiah, chap. liii. ver. 4, which is as follows:

"Surely *he* (the person of whom Isaiah is speaking) *hath borne* our griefs and carried our sorrows." It is in the preter tense.

Here is nothing about casting out devils, nor curing of sicknesses. The passage, therefore, so far from being a pro‑ phecy of Christ, is not even applicable as a circumstance.

Isaiah, or at least the writer of the book that bears his name, employs the whole of this chapter, the 53d, in lament‑ ing the sufferings of some deceased person, of whom he speaks very pathetically. It is a monody on the death of a friend; but he mentions not the name of the person, nor gives any circumstance of him by which he can be personally known; and it is this silence, which is evidence of nothing, that Matthew has laid hold of to put the name of Christ to it; as if the chiefs of the Jews, whose sorrows were then great, and the times they lived in big with danger, were never thinking about their own affairs, nor the fate of their own friends, but were continually running a wild-goose chase into futurity.

To make a monody into a prophecy is an absurdity. The characters and circumstances of men, even in different ages of the world, are so much a like, that what is said of one may with propriety be said of many; but this fitness does not make the passage into a prophecy; and none but an impostor or a bigot would call it so.

Isaiah, in deploring the hard fate and loss of his friend, mentions nothing of him but what the human lot of man is subject to. All the cases he states of him, his persecutions, his imprisonment, his patience in suffering, and his perse‑ verance in principle, are all within the line of nature; they belong exclusively to none, and may with justness be said of many. But if Jesus Christ was the person the church represents him to be, that which would exclusively apply to him, must be something that could not apply to any other person; something beyond the line of nature; something beyond the lot of mortal man; and there are no such expressions in this chapter, nor any other chapter in the Old Testament.

It is no exclusive description to say of a person, as is said of the person, Isaiah is lamenting in this chapter. "*He was oppressed and he was afflicted, yet he opened not his mouth: he is brought as a Lamb to the slaughter, and as a sheep before his shearers is dumb, so he opened not his mouth.*" This may be said of thousands of persons, who have suffered oppression and unjust death with patience, silence, and perfect resignation.

Grotius, whom the bishop esteems a most learned man, and who certainly was so, supposes that the person of whom Isaiah is speaking, is Jeremiah. Grotius is led into this opinion, from the agreement there is between the description given by Isaiah, and the case of Jeremiah, as stated in the book that bears his name. If Jeremiah was an innocent man, and not a traitor in the interest of Nebuchadnezzer, when Jerusalem was besieged, his case was hard; he was accused by his countrymen, was persecuted, oppressed, and imprisoned, and he says of himself (see Jeremiah, chap. ii. ver. 19,) "*But as for me, I was like a lamb or an ox that is brought to the slaughter.*"

I should be inclined to the same opinion with Grotius, had Isaiah lived at the time when Jeremiah underwent the cruelties of which he speaks; but Isaiah died about fifty years before; and it is of a person of his own time, whose case Isaiah is lamenting in the chapter in question, and which imposition and bigotry, more than seven hundred years afterwards, perverted into a prophecy of a person they call Jesus Christ.

I pass on to the eighth passage called a prophecy of Jesus Christ.

Matthew, chap. xii. ver. 14. "Then the Pharisees went out and held a council against him, how they might destroy him—But when Jesus knew it he withdrew himself; and great numbers followed him and he healed them all—and he charged them they should not make him known: That it might be fulfilled which was spoken by Esaias (Isaiah) the prophet, saying,

" Behold my servant whom I have chosen; my beloved in whom my soul is well pleased, I will put my spirit upon him, and he shall shew judgment to the Gentiles—he shall not strive nor cry, neither shall any man hear his voice in the street—a bruised reed shall he not break, and smoaking flax shall he not quench till he sends forth judgment unto victory—and in his name shall the Gentiles trust."

In the first place, this passage hath not the least relation to the purpose for which it is quoted.

Matthew says, that the Pharisees held a council against Jesus to destroy him—that Jesus withdrew himself—that great numbers followed him—that he healed them—and that he charged them they should not make him known.

But the passage Matthew has quoted as being fulfilled by these circumstances, does not so much as apply to any one of them. It has nothing to do with the Pharisees holding a council to destroy Jesus—with his withdrawing himself—with great numbers following him—with his healing them—nor with his charging them not to make him known.

The purpose for which the passage is quoted, and the passage itself, are as remote from each other, as nothing from something. But the case is, that people have been so long in the habit of reading the books called the Bible and Testament, with their eyes shut, and their senses locked up, that the most stupid inconsistences have passed on them for truths, and imposition for prophecy. The all-wise Creator hath been dishonoured by being made the author of fable, and the human mind degraded by believing it.

In this passage, as in that last mentioned, the name of the person of whom the passage speaks is not given, and we are left in the dark respecting him. It is this defect in the history, that bigotry and imposition have laid hold of, to call it prophecy.

Had Isaiah lived in the time of Cyrus, the passage would descriptively apply to him. As king of Persia, his authority was great among the Gentiles, and it is of such a character the passage speaks; and his friendship to the Jews whom he liberated from captivity, and who might then be compared to a *bruised reed*, was extensive. But this description does not apply to Jesus Christ, who had no authority among the Gentiles; and as to his own countrymen, figuratively described by the bruised reed, it was they who crucified him. Neither can it be said of him that he did not cry, and that his voice was not heard in the street. As a preacher it was his business to be heard, and we are told that he travelled about the country for that purpose. Matthew has given a long sermon, which (if his authority is good, but which is much to be doubted, since he imposes so much,) Jesus preached to a multitude upon a mountain, and it would be a quibble to say that a mountain is not a street, since it is a place equally as public.

The last verse in the passage (the 4th), as it stands in Isaiah, and which Matthew has not quoted, says, " He shall not fail nor be discouraged till he have set judgment in the earth and the isles shall wait for his law." This also applies to Cyrus. He was not discouraged, he did not fail, he conquered all Babylon, liberated the Jews, and established laws. But this cannot be said of Jesus Christ, who, in the passage before us, according to Matthew, withdrew himself for fear of the Pharisees, and charged the people that followed him not to make it known where he was; and who, according to other parts of the Testament, was continually moving from place to place to avoid being apprehended.*

---

* In the second part of the *Age of Reason*, I have shewn that the book ascribed to Isaiah is not only miscellaneous as to matter, but as to authorship; that there are parts in it which could not be written by Isaiah, because they speak of things one hundred and fifty years after he was dead. The instance I have given of this, in that work, corresponds with the subject I am upon, *at least a little better than Matthew's introduction and his quotation.*

Isaiah lived, the latter part of his life, in the time of Hezekiah, and it was about one hundred and fifty years from the death of Hezekiah to the first year of the reign of Cyrus, when Cyrus published a proclamation, which is given in the first chapter of the book of Ezra, for the return of the Jews to Jerusalem. It cannot be doubted, at least it ought not to be doubted, that the Jews would feel an affectionate gratitude for this act of benevolent justice, and it is natural they would express that gratitude in the customary style, bombastical and hyperbolical as it was, which they used on extraordinary occasions, and which was, and still is in practice with all the eastern nations.

The instance to which I refer, and which is given in the second part of the Age of Reason, is the last verse of the 44th chapter and the beginning of the 45th—in these words: " *That saith of Cyrus he is my shepherd and shall perform all my pleasure: even saying to Jerusalem thou shalt be built, and to the Temple, thy foundation shalt be laid. Thus saith the Lord to his anointed, to Cyrus, whose right hand I have holden to subdue nations before him; and I will loose the loins of kings, to open before him the two-leaved gates, and the gates shall not be shut.*

This complimentary address is in the present tense, which shews that the things of which it speaks were in existence at the time of writing it; and consequently, that the author must have been at

But it is immaterial to us, at this distance of time, to know who the person was: it is sufficient to the purpose I am upon, that of detecting fraud and falsehood, to know who it was not, and to shew it was not the person called Jesus Christ.

I pass on to the ninth passage called a prophecy of Jesus Christ

Matthew, chap. xxi. v. 1. "And when they drew nigh unto Jerusalem, and were come to Bethphage, unto the mount of Olives, then Jesus sent two of his disciples, saying unto them, go into the village over against you, and straightway ye shall find an ass tied, and a colt with her, loose them and bring them unto me—and if any man say aught to you, ye shall say, the Lord hath need of them, and straightway he will send them.

" All this was done that it might be fulfilled which was spoken by the prophet, saying, *Tell ye the daughter of Sion, behold thy king cometh unto thee meek, and setting on an ass, and a colt the foal of an ass.*

Poor ass! let it be some consolation amidst all thy sufferings, that if the heathen world erected a bear into a constellation, the Christian world has elevated thee into a prophecy.

This passage is in Zechariah, chap. ix. ver. 9, and is one of the whims of friend Zechariah to congratulate his countrymen, who were then returning from captivity in Babylon, and himself with them, to Jerusalem. It has no concern with any other subject. It is strange that apostles, priests, or commentators, never permit, or never suppose, the Jews, to be speaking of their own affairs. Every thing in the Jewish books is perverted and distorted into meanings never

---

leat one hundred and fifty years later than Isaiah, and that the book which bears his name is a compilation. The Proverbs called Solomon's and the Psalms called David's, are of the same kind. The two last verses of the second book of Chronicles, and the three first verses of the first chapter of Ezra, are word for word the same; which shew that the compilers of the Bible mixed the writings of different authors together, and put them under some common head.

As we have here an instance, in the 44th and 45th chapters, of the introduction of the name of Cyrus into a book to which it cannot belong, it affords good ground to conclude, that the passage in the 42d chapter, in which the character of Cyrus is given without his name, has been introduced in like manner, and that the person there spoken of is Cyrus.

intended by the writers. Even the poor ass must not be a
Jew-ass but a Christian-ass. I wonder they did not make
an apostle of him, or a bishop, or at least make him speak
and prophecy. He could have lifted up his voice as loud
as any of them.

Zechariah, in the first chapter of his book, indulges himself in several whims on the joy of getting back to Jerusalem. He says at the 8th verse, " I saw by night (Zechariah
was a sharp-sighted seer) and behold a man sitting on a *red
horse*, (yes, reader, a *red horse*) and he stood among the
myrtle trees that were in the bottom, and behind him were
red horses speckled and white. He says nothing about green
horses, nor blue horses, perhaps because it is difficult to distinguish green from blue by night, but a Christian can have
no doubt they were there, because "*faith is the evidence of
things not seen*."

Zechariah then introduces an angel among his horses, but
he does not tell us what colour the angel was of, whether
black or white, nor whether he came to buy horses, or only
to look at them as curiosities, for certainly they were of that
kind. Be this, however, as it may, he enters into conversation with this angel, on the joyful affair of getting back to
Jerusalem, and he saith at the 16th verse, " *Therefore thus
saith the Lord*, I AM RETURNED *to Jerusalem with mer-
cies ; my house shall be built in it saith the Lord of hosts,
and a line shall be stretched forth upon Jerusalem*." An expression signifying the rebuilding the city.

All this, whimsical and imaginary as it is, sufficiently
proves that it was the entry of the Jews into Jerusalem from
captivity, and not the entry of Jesus Christ seven hundred
years afterwards, that is the subject upon which Zechariah
is always speaking.

As to the expression of riding upon an ass, which commentators represent as a sign of humility in Jesus Christ,
the case is, he never was so well mounted before. The asses
of those countries are large and well-proportioned, and were
anciently the chief of riding animals. Their beasts of bur-
den, and which served also for the conveyance of the poor,
were camels and dromedaries. We read in Judges, chap.
x. ver. 4, that " Jair (one of the Judges of Israel) had thirty
sons that rode on *thirty ass-colts*, and they had thirty cities."
But commentators distort every thing.

There is besides very reasonable grounds to conclude
that this story of Jesus riding publicly into Jerusalem,
accompanied, as it is said at the 8th and 9th verses, by a

great multitude, shouting and rejoicing and spreading their garments by the way, is altogether a story destitute of truth.

In the last passage called a prophecy that I examined, Jesus is represented as withdrawing, that is, running away, and concealing himself for fear of being apprehended, and charging the people that were with him not to make him known. No new circumstances had risen in the interim to change his condition for the better; yet here he is represented as making his public entry into the same city from which he had fled for safety. The two cases contradict each other so much, that if both are not false, one of them at least can scarcely be true. For my own part, I do not believe there is one word of historical truth in the whole book. I look upon it at best to be a romance; the principal personage of which is an imaginary or allegorical character founded upon some tale, and in which the moral is in many parts good, and the narrative part very badly and blunderingly written.

I pass on to the tenth passage, called a prophecy of Jesus Christ.

Matthew, chap. xxvi. ver. 51. " And behold one of them which was with Jesus (meaning Peter) stretched out his hand, and drew his sword, and struck a servant of the high priest, and smote off his ear. Then said Jesus unto him, Put up again thy sword into its place, for all they that take the sword shall perish with the sword. Thinkest thou that I cannot now pray to my father, and he shall presently give me more than twelve legions of angels. But how then shall the scriptures be fulfilled that thus it must be. In that same hour Jesus said to the multitudes, are ye come out as against a thief with swords and with staves for to take me? I sat daily with you teaching in the temple, and ye laid no hold on me. But all this was done that the scriptures of the prophets might be fulfilled.

This loose and general manner of speaking, admits neither of detection nor of proof. Here is no quotation given, nor the name of any Bible author mentioned, to which reference can be had.

There are, however, some high improbabilities against the truth of the account.

First—It is not probable that the Jews, who were then a conquered people, and under subjection to the Romans, should be permitted to wear swords.

Secondly—If Peter had attacked the servant of the high

priest and cut off his ear, he would have been immediately taken up by the guard that took up his master, and sent to prison with him.

Thirdly—What sort of disciples and preaching apostles must those of Christ have been that wore swords?

Fourthly—This scene is represented to have taken place the same evening of what is called the Lord's Supper, which makes, according to the ceremony of it, the inconsistency of wearing swords the greater.

I pass on to the eleventh passage called a prophecy of Jesus Christ.

Matthew, chap. xxvii. ver. 3. " Then Judas which had betrayed him, when he saw that he was condemned, repented himself, and brought again the thirty pieces of silver to the chief priests and elders, saying, I have sinned in that I have betrayed the innocent blood. And they said, what is that to us, see thou to that. And he cast down the pieces of silver, and departed and went and hanged himself—And the chief priests took the silver pieces and said, it is not lawful to put them in the treasury, because it is the price of blood —And they took counsel and bought with them the potters field to bury strangers in—Wherefore that field is called the field of blood unto this day. Then was fulfilled that which was spoken by Jeremiah the prophet, saying, And they took the thirty pieces of silver, the price of him that was valued, whom they of the children of Israel did value, and gave them for the potters field, as the Lord appointed me."

This is a most bare-faced piece of imposition. The passage in Jeremiah which speaks of the purchaser of a field, has no more to do with the case to which Matthew applies it, than it has to do with the purchase of lands in America. I will recite the whole passage ;

Jeremiah, chap. xxxii. v. 6. "And Jeremiah said, the word of the Lord came unto me, saying—Behold Hanamiel the son of Shallum thine uncle shall come unto thee, saying buy thee my field that is in Anathoth, for the right of redemption is thine to buy it—So Hanamiel mine uncle's son came to me in the court of the prison, according to the word of the Lord, and said unto me, buy my field I pray thee, that is in Anathoth, which is in the country of Benjamin, for the right of inheritance is thine, and the redemption is thine; buy it for thyself. Then I knew this was the word of the Lord—And I bought the field of Hanamiel mine uncle's son that was in Anathoth, and weighed him the money, even seventeen shekels of silver—and I subscribed the evidence and sealed it, and took witnesses and weighed hi_ _ _ _ _

ney in balances. So I took the evidence of the purchase,
both that which was sealed according to the law and cus-
tom, and that which was open—and I gave the evidence of
the purchase unto Baruch, the son of Neriah, the-son of
Maaseiath, in the sight of Hanamiel mine uncle's son, and
in the presence of the witnesses that subscribed, before all
the Jews that sat in the court of the prison—and I charged
Baruch before them, saying, Thus saith the Lord of hosts,
the God of Israel, Take these evidences, this evidence of the
purchase, both which is sealed, and this evidence which is
open, and put them in an earthen vessel, that they may continue many days—for thus saith the Lord of hosts, the God
of Israel, houses, and fields, and vineyards, shall be possessed again in this land."

I forbear making any remark on this abominable imposition of Matthew. The thing glaringly speaks for itself. It
is priests and commentators that I rather ought to censure,
for having preached falsehood so long, and kept people in
darkness with respect to those impositions. I am not con-
tending with these men upon points of doctrine, for I know
that sophistry has always a city of refuge. I am speaking
of facts; for wherever the thing called a fact is a falsehood,
the faith founded upon it is delusion, and the doctrine raised
upon it not true. Ah, reader, put thy trust in thy Creator,
and thou wilt be safe: but if thou trustest to the book called
the Scriptures, thou trustest to the rotten staff of fable and
falsehood. But I return to my subject.

' There is among the whims and reveries of Zechariah, mention made of thirty pieces of silver given to a potter. They
can hardly have been so stupid as to mistake a potter for a
field; and if they had, the passage in Zechariah has no more
to do with Jesus, Judas. and the field to bury strangers in,
than that already quoted. I will recite the passage.

Zechariah, chap. xi. ver. 7. "And I will feed the flock
of slaughter, even you, O poor of the flock; and I took unto
me two staves; the one I called *Beauty* and the other 1
called *Bands*, and 1 fed the flock   Three shepherds also, I
cut off in one month ; and my soul loathed them, and their
soul also abhorred me. Then said I, I will not feed you ;
that which dieth, let it die: and that which is to be cut off,
let it be cut off; and let the rest eat every one the flesh of
another. And I took my staff, even *Beauty*, and cut it
asunder, that I might break my covenant which I had made
with all the people. And it was broken in that day ; and so
the poor of the flock who waited upon me, knew that it was
the word of the Lord.

"And I said unto them, if ye think good give me my price, and if not, forbear. So they weighed for my price *thirty pieces of silver*. And the Lord said unto me, cast it unto the potter, a goodly price that I was prized at of them; and I took the thirty pieces of silver and cast them to the potter in the house of the Lord.

"When I cut asunder mine other staff, even *Bands*, that I might break the brotherhood between Judah and Israel."*

There is no making either head or tail of this incoherent gibberish. His two staves, one called *Beauty* and the other *Bands*, is so much like a fairy tale, that I doubt if it had any higher origin. There is, however, no part that has the least relation to the case stated in Matthew: on the con-

---

* Whiston, in his Essay on the Old Testament, says, that the passage of Zechariah of which I have spoken, was in the copies of the Bible of the first century, in the book of Jeremiah, from whence, says he, it was taken and inserted without coherence, in that of Zechariah—well, let it be so, it does not make the case a whit the better for the New Testament; but it makes the case a great deal the worse for the Old. Because it shews, as I have mentioned respecting some passages in a book ascribed to Isaiah, that the works of different authors have been so mixed and confounded together, they cannot now be discriminated, except where they are historical chronological, or biographical, as is the interpolation in Isaiah. It is the name of Cyrus inserted where it could not be inserted, as he was not in existence till one hundred and fifty years after the time of Isaiah, that detects the interpolation and the blunder with it.

Whiston was a man of great literary learning, and, what is of much higher degree, of deep scientific learning. He was one of the best and most celebrated mathematicians of his time, for which he was made Professor of Mathematics of the University of Cambridge. He wrote so much in the defence of the Old Testament, and of what he calls prophecies of Jesus Christ, that at last he began to suspect the truth of the Scriptures, and wrote against them; for it is only those who examine them that see the imposition. Those who believe them most are those who know least about them.

Whiston, after writing so much in defence of the Scriptures, was at last prosecuted for writing against them. It was this that gave occasion to Swift, in his ludicrious epigram on Ditton and Whiston, each of which set up to find out the longitude, to call the one *good master Ditton*, and the other *wicked Will Whiston*. But as Swift was a great associate with the Freethinkers of those days, such as Bolingbroke, Pope, and others, who did not believe the books called the Scriptures, there is no certainty whether he wittily called him *wicked* for defending the Scriptures, or for writing against them. The known character of Swift decides for the former.

3

trary, it is the reverse of it. Here the *thirty pieces* of silver
whatever it was for, is called a *goodly price*, (it was as much
as the thing was worth,) and according to the language of
the day, was approved of by the Lord, and the money given
to the potter in the house of the Lord. In the case of Jesus
and Judas, as stated in Matthew, the thirty pieces of silver
were the price of blood; the transaction was condemned by
the Lord, and the money, when refunded, was refused admit-
tance into the treasury. Every thing in the two cases is the
reverse of each other.

Besides this, a very different and direct contrary account
to that of Matthew, is given of the affair of Judas, in the
book called the *Acts of the Apostles*; according to that book
the case is, that so far from Judas repenting and returning
the money, and the high priest buying a field with it to bury
strangers in, Judas kept the money and bought a field with
it for himself; and instead of hanging himself as Matthew
says, that he fell headlong and burst asunder—some commentators endeavour to get over one part of the contradiction by ridiculously supposing that Judas hanged himself
first and the rope broke.

Acts, chap. i. ver. 16. "Men and brethren, this scripture
must needs have been fulfilled which the Holy Ghost by the
mouth of David spake before concerning Judas, which was a
guide to them that took Jesus. (David says not a word
about Judas) ver. 17, for he (Judas) was numbered among
us and obtained part of our ministry."

Ver. 18. " Now this man purchased a field with the reward
of iniquity, and falling headlong he burst asunder in the midst,
and his bowels gushed out." Is it not a species of blasphemy
to call the New Testament *revealed religion*, when we see in
it such contradictions and absurdities.

I pass on to the twelfth passage called a prophecy of
Jesus Christ.

Matthew, chap. xxvii. ver. 35. "And they crucified him
and parted his garments, casting lots; that it might be fulfilled which was spoken by the prophet, *They parted my garments among them, and upon my vesture did they cast lots.*"
This expression is in the 22d Psalm, ver. xviii. The writer
of that Psalm, (whoever he was, for the Psalms are a collection and not the work of one man) is speaking of himself
and of his own case, and not of that of another. He begins
this Psalm with the words which the New Testament writers
ascribed to Jesus Christ. "*My God, my God, why hast
thou forsaken me*"—words which might be uttered by a com-

plaining man without any great impropriety, but very im-.
properly from the mouth of a reputed God.

The picture which the writer draws of his own situation
in this Psalm, is gloomy enough. He is not prophesying,
but complaining of his own hard case. He represents himself as surrounded by enemies and beset by persecutions of
every kind; and by way of shewing the inveteracy of his
persecutors, he says at the 18th verse, " *They parted my garments among them, and cast lots upon my vesture.*" The expression is in the present tense; and is the same as to say,
they pursue me even to the clothes upon my back, and dispute how they shall divide them ; besides, the word *vesture*
does not always mean clothing of any kind, but *property*,
or rather the admitting a man to, or *investing* him with property : and as it is used in this Psalm distinct from the word
garment, it appears to be used in this sense. But Jesus had
no property ; for they make him say of himself, " The foxes
have holes and the birds of the air have nests, but the Son of
man hath no where to lay his head."

But be this as it may, if we permit ourselves to suppose
the Almighty would condescend to tell, by what is called
the spirit of prophecy, what would come to pass in some
future age of the world, it is an injury to our own faculties,
and to our ideas of his greatness, to imagine it would be
about an old coat, or an old pair of breeches, or about any
thing which the common accidents of life, or the quarrels
that attend it, exhibit every day.

That which is within the power of man to do, or in his
will not to do, is not a subject for prophecy, even if there
were such a thing, because it cannot carry with it any evidence of divine power, or divine interposition. The ways
of God are not the ways of men. That which an Almighty
Power performs, or wills, is not within the circle of human
power to do, or to controul. But any executioner and his
assistants might quarrel about dividing the garments of a
sufferer, or divide them without quarrelling, and by that
means fulfil the thing called a prophecy, or set it aside,

In the passages before examined, I have exposed the falsehood of them. In this I exhibit its degrading meanness
as an insult to the Creator and an injury to human
reason.

Here end the passages called prophecies by Matthew.

Matthew concludes his book by saying, that when Christ
expired on the cross, the rocks rent, the graves opened, and
the bodies of many of the saints arose; and Mark says,
there was darkness over the land from the sixth hour until

, the ninth They produce no prophecy for this; but had these things been facts, they would have been a proper subject for prophecy, because none but an Almighty Power could have inspired a fore-knowledge of them, and afterwards fulfilled them. Since then, there is no such prophecy, but a pretended prophecy of an old coat, the proper deduction is, there were no such things, and that the book of Matthew is fable and falsehood.

I pass on to the book called the Gospel according to St. Mark.

THE BOOK OF MARK.

THERE are but few passages in Mark called prophecies, and but few in Luke and John. Such as there are I shall examine, and also such other passages as interfere with those cited by Matthew.

Mark begins his book by a passage which he puts in the shape of a prophecy. Mark, chap. i. ver. 1.—" The beginning of the Gospel of Jesus Christ, the son of God—As it is written in the prophets, *Behold I send my messenger before thy face, which shall prepare the way before thee;*" (Malachi, chap. iii. ver. 1.) The passage in the original is in the first person. Mark makes this passage to be a prophecy of John the Baptist, said by the Church to be a forerunner of Jesus Christ. But if we attend to the verses that follow this expression, as it stands in Malachi, and to the first and fifth verses of the next chapter, we shall see that this application of it is erroneous and false.

Malachi having said at the first verse, " Behold I will send my messenger, and he shall prepare the way before me, says at the second verse, " *But who may abide the day of his coming; and who shall stand when he appeareth? for he is like a refiner's fire, and like fuller's soap.*"

This description can have no reference to the birth of Jesus Christ, and consequently none to John the Baptist. It is a scene of fear and terror that is here described, and the birth of Christ is always spoken of as a time of joy and glad tidings.

Malachi, continuing to speak on the same subject, explains in the next chapter what the scene is of which he speaks in the verses above quoted, and who the person is whom he calls the messenger.

" Behold," says he, chap. iv. ver. 1, " the day cometh that shall burn like an oven, and all the proud, yea, and all that do wickedly, shall be stubble; and the day cometh that shall burn them up, saith the Lord of hosts, that it shall leave them neither root nor branch."

Ver. 5. " Behold 1 will send you Elijah the prophet, before the coming of the great and dreadful day of the Lord."

By what right, or by what imposition or ignorance, Mark has made Elijah into John the Baptist, and Malachi's description of the day of judgment into the birth-day of Christ, I leave to the Bishop to settle.

Mark, in the second and third verses of his first chapter, confounds two passages together, taken from different books of the Old Testament. The second verse, " *Behold I send my messenger before thy face, which shall prepare the way before thee,*" is taken as I have before said, from Malachi. The third verse, which says, " *The voice of one crying in the wilderness, prepare ye the way of the Lord, make his path straight,*" is not in Malachi, but in Isaiah, chap. xl. ver. 3. Whiston says, that both these verses were originally in Isaiah. If so, it is another instance of the disordered state of the Bible, and corroborates what I have said with respect to the name and description of Cyrus being in the book of Isaiah, to which it cannot chronologically belong.

The words in Isaiah, chap. xl. ver. 3, " The voice of him that cryeth in the wilderness, prepare ye the way of the Lord, make his path straight," are in the present tense, and consequently not predictive. It is one of those rhetorical figures which the Old Testament authors frequently used. That it is merely rhetorical and metaphorical, may be seen at the 6th verse—" And the voice said, cry; and he said, what shall I cry? *All flesh is grass.*" This is evidently nothing but a figure; for flesh is not grass otherwise than as a figure or metaphor, where one thing is put for another. Besides which, the whole passage is too general and declamatory to be applied exclusively to any particular person or purpose.

I pass on to the eleventh chapter.

In this chapter Mark speaks of Christ riding into Jerusalem upon a colt, but he does not make it the accomplishment of a prophecy, as Matthew has done; for he says nothing about a prophecy. Instead of which, he goes on the other tack, and in order to add new honours to the ass, he makes it to be a miracle; for he says, ver. 2, it was " *a colt whereon never man sat,*" signifying thereby, that as the ass had not been broken, he consequently was inspired *into good manners,* for we do not hear that he kicked Jesus Christ off.

There is not a word about his kicking in all the four Evangelists.

I pass on from these feats of *horsemanship*, performed upon a jack-ass, to the 15th chapter.

At the 24th verse of this chapter, Mark speaks of *parting Christ's garments and casting lots upon them*, but he applies no prophecy to it as Matthew does. He rather speaks of it as a thing then in practice with executioners, as it is at this day.

At the 28th verse of the same chapter, Mark speaks of Christ being crucified between two thieves, that, says he, " *the Scriptures might be fulfilled, which saith, And he was numbered with the transgressors.*" The same thing might be said of the thieves.

This expression is in Isaiah, chap. liii. ver. 12. Grotius applies it to Jeremiah. But the case has happened so often in the world, where innocent men have been numbered with transgressors, and is still continually happening, that it is absurdity to call it a prophecy of any particular person. All those whom the Church calls martyrs were numbered with transgressors. All the honest patriots who fell upon the scaffold in France, in the time of Robespierre, were numbered with transgressors; and if himself had not fallen, the same case, according to a note in his own hand-writing, had befallen me; yet I suppose the Bishop will not allow that Isaiah was prophesying of Thomas Paine.

These are all the passages in Mark which have any reference to prophecies.

Mark concludes his book by making Jesus to say to his disciples, chap. xvi. ver. 15, " Go ye into all the world and preach the Gospel to every creature; he that believeth and is baptized shall be saved, but he that believeth not shall be damned (fine Popish stuff this), and these signs shall follow them that believe—in my name they shall cast out devils; they shall speak with new tongues; they shall take up serpents; and if they drink any deadly thing it shall not hurt them; they shall lay hands on the sick and they shall recover."

Now, the Bishop, in order to know if he has all this saving and wonder-working faith, should try those things upon himself. He should take a good dose of arsenic, and if he please, I will send him a rattle-snake from America! As for myself, as I believe in God, and not at all in Jesus Christ, nor in the books called the Scriptures, the experiment does not concern me.

I pass on to the book of Luke.

THE BOOK OF LUKE.

THERE are no passages in Luke called prophecies except-ing those which relate to the passages I have already ex-amined.

Luke speaks of Mary being espoused to Joseph, but he makes no references to the passages in Isaiah, as Matthew does. He speaks also of Jesus riding into Jerusalem upon a colt, but he says nothing about a prophecy. He speaks of John the Baptist, and refers to the passage in Isaiah of which I have already spoken.

At the 13th chapter, verse 31, he says, " The same day there came certain of the Pharisees, saying unto him (Jesus) get thee out and depart hence, for Herod will kill thee—and he said unto them, go ye and tell that Fox, behold I cast out devils and I do cures to-day and to-morrow, and the third day I shall be perfected."

Matthew makes Herod to die whilst Christ was a child in Egypt, and makes Joseph to return with the child on the news of Herod's death, who had sought to kill him. Luke makes Herod to be living and to seek the life of Jesus after Jesus was thirty years of age; for he says, chap. iii. v. 23, " And Jesus began to be about thirty years of age, being, as was supposed, the son of Joseph."

The obscurity in which the historical part of the New Testament is involved with respect to Herod, may afford to priests and commentators a plea, which to some may appear plausible, but to none satisfactory, that the Herod of which Matthew speaks, and the Herod of which Luke speaks, were different persons. Matthew calls Herod a king; and Luke, chap. iii. v. 1, calls Herod, Tetrarch (that is, Go-vernor) of Galilee. But there could be no such person as *a king* Herod, because the Jews and their country were then under the dominion of the Roman Emperors, who govern-ed them by Tetrarchs or Governors.

Luke, chap. ii. makes Jesus to be born when Cyrenius was Governor of Syria, to which government Judea was annexed; and according to this, Jesus was not born in the time of Herod. Luke says nothing about Herod seeking the life of Jesus when he was born; nor of his destroying the children under two years old; nor of Joseph fleeing with Jesus into Egypt; nor of his returning from thence. On the contrary, the book of Luke speaks as if the person it calls Christ had never been out of Judea, and that Herod sought his life after he commenced preaching, as is before stated. I have already shewn that Luke, in the book called the Acts of the Apostles, (which commentators ascribe to Luke) contradicts the account in Matthew, with respect to Judas and the thirty pieces of silver. Matthew says, that Judas returned the money, and that the high priest bought with it a field to bury strangers in. Luke says, that Judas kept the money and bought a field with it for himself.

As it is impossible the wisdom of God could err, so it is impossible those books could have been written by divine inspiration. Our belief in God, and his unerring wisdom, forbids us to believe it. As for myself, I feel religiously happy in the total disbelief of it.

There are no other passages called prophecies in Luke than those I have spoken of. I pass on to the book of John.

THE BOOK OF JOHN.

JOHN, like Mark and Luke, is not much of a prophecy-monger. He speaks of the ass, and the casting lots for Jesus's clothes, and some other trifles, of which I have already spoken.

John makes Jesus to say, chap. v. ver. 46, " For had ye believed Moses, ye would have believed me, for he wrote of me." The book of the Acts, in speaking of Jesus, says, chap. iii. ver. 22, " For Moses truly said unto the fathers, a prophet shall the Lord God raise up unto you, of your brethren, like unto me, him shall ye hear in all things what-soever he shall say unto you."

This passage is in Deuteronomy, chap. xviii. ver. 15. They apply it as a prophecy of Jesus. What imposition! The person spoken of in Deuteronomy, and also in Num-bers where the same person is also spoken of, is *Joshua*, the minister of Moses, and his immediate successor, and just such another Robespierrean character as Moses is represented to have been. The case, as related in those books, is as follows:—

Moses was grown old and near to his end, and in order to prevent confusion after his death, (for the Israelites had no settled system of government) it was thought best to nominate a successor to Moses while he was yet living. This was done, as we are told, in the following manner:

Numbers, chap. xxvii. ver. 12. " And the Lord said unto Moses, get thee up into this mount Abarim, and see the land which I have given unto the children of Israel—and when thou hast seen it, thou also shall be gathered unto thy people as Aaron thy brother is gathered, ver. 15. And Moses spake unto the Lord, saying, Let the Lord, the God of the spirit of all flesh, set a man over the congregation—Which may go out before them, and which may go in before them, and which may lead them out, and which may bring them in, that the congregation of the Lord be not as sheep that have no shepherd—And the Lord said unto Moses, take thee *Joshua*, the son of Nun, a man in whom is the spirit, and lay thine hand upon him—and set him before Eleazar, the priest, and before all the congregation, and give him a charge in their sight—and thou shalt put some of thine honour upon him, and that all the congregation of the children of Israel may be obedient, ver. 22, and Moses did as the Lord commanded, and he took Joshua, and set him before Eleazar the priest, and before all the congregation; and he laid hands upon him, and gave him charge as the Lord commanded by the hand of Moses."

I have nothing to do, in this place, with the truth, or the conjuration here practised, of raising up a successor to Moses like unto himself. The passage sufficiently proves it is Joshua, and that it is an imposition in John to make the case into a prophecy of Jesus. But the prophecy-mongers were so inspired with falsehood, that they never speak truth.*

---

* Newton, Bishop of Bristol in England, published a work in three volumes, entitled, " *Dissertations on the Prophecies.*" The work is tediously written and tiresome to read. He strains hard to make 'every passage into a prophecy that suits his purpose. Among others, he makes this expression of Moses, " the Lord shall raise thee up a prophet like unto me," into a prophecy of Christ, who was not born, according to the Bible chronologies, till fifteen hundred and fifty-two years after the time of Moses, whereas it was an immediate successor to Moses, who was then near his end, that is spoken of in the passage above quoted.

I pass on to the last passage in these fables of the Evangelists, called a prophecy of Jesus Christ.

John having spoken of Jesus expiring on the cross between two thieves, says, chap. xix. ver. 32, " Then came

---

This Bishop, the better to impose this passage on the world as a prophecy of Christ, has entirely omitted the account in the book of Numbers which I have given at length word for word, and which shews, beyond the possibility of a doubt, that the person spoken of by Moses, is Joshua, and no other person.

Newton is but a superficial writer. He takes up things upon *hear say*, and inserts them without either examination or reflection, and the more extraordinary and incredible they are, the better he likes them.

In speaking of the walls of Babylon, (volume the first, page 263,) he makes a quotation from a traveller of the name of *Tavernur*, whom he calls (by the way of giving credit to what he says) *a celebrated traveller*, that those walls *were made of burnt brick, ten feet square and three feet thick.* If Newton had only thought of calculating the weight of such a brick, he would have seen the impossibility of their being used or even made. A brick ten feet square, and three feet thick, contains 300 cubic feet, and allowing a cubic foot of brick to be only one hundred pounds, each of the Bishop's bricks would weigh thirty thousand pounds; and it would take about thirty cart-loads of clay (one-horse carts) to make one brick.

But his account of the stones used in the building of Solomon's temple (volume 2d, page 211,) far exceeds his bricks of ten feet square in the walls of Babylon, these are but brick-bats compared to them.

The stones (says he) employed in the foundation, were in magnitude forty cubits, that is, above sixty feet, a cubit, says he, being somewhat more than one foot and a half, (a cubit is one foot nine inches) and the superstructure (says this Bishop) was worthy of such foundations. There were some stones, say he, of the whitest marble, forty-five cubits long, five cubits high, and six cubits broad These are the dimensions this Bishop has given, which in measure of twelve inches to a foot, is 78 feet 9 inches long, 10 feet 6 inches broad, and 8 feet three inches thick, and contains 7,234 cubic feet. I now go to demonstrate the imposition of this Bishop.

A cubic foot of water weighs sixty-two pounds and a-half. The specific gravity of marble to water is as 2 1-2 is to one. The weight therefore of a cubic foot of marble is 156 pounds, which, multiplied by 7,234, the number of cubic feet in one of those stones, makes the weight of it to be 1,128,504 pounds, which is 503 tons. Allowing then a horse to draw about half a ton, it will require a thousand horses to draw one such a stone on the ground; how then were they to be lifted into the building by human hands?

the soldiers and brake the legs of the first (meaning one of the thieves) and of the other which was crucified with him. But when they came to Jesus and saw that he was dead already, they brake not his legs—ver. 36, for these things were done that the Scripture should be fulfilled, " *A bone of him shall not be broken.*"

The passage here referred to is in Exodus, and has no more to do with Jesus than with the ass he rode upon to Jerusalem;—nor yet so much, if a roasted jack-ass, like a roasted he-goat, might be eaten at a Jewish passover. It might be some consolation to an ass to know, that though his bones might be picked, they would not be broken. I go to state the case.

The book of Exodus, in instituting the Jewish passover, in which they were to eat a he-lamb or a he-goat, says, chap. xii. ver. 5, " Your lamb shall be without blemish, a male of the first year; ye shall take it from the *sheep* or from the *goats.*"

The book, after stating some ceremonies to be used in killing and dressing it, (for it was to be roasted, not boiled) says, ver. 43, " And the Lord said unto Moses and Aaron, this is the ordinance of the passover : there shall no stranger eat thereof; but every man's servant that is bought for money, when thou hast circumcised him, then shall he eat thereof. A foreigner shall not eat thereof. In one house shall it be eaten : thou shalt not carry forth aught of the

---

The Bishop may talk of faith removing mountains, but all the faith of all the Bishops that ever lived could not remove one of those stones and their bodily strength given in.

This Bishop also tells of *great guns* used by the Turks at the taking of Constantinople, one of which, he says, was drawn by seventy yoke of oxen, and by two thousand men. Volume 3d, page 117.

The weight of a cannon that carries a ball of 48 pounds, which is the largest cannon that are cast, weighs 8,000 pounds, about three tons and a half, and may be drawn by three yoke of oxen. Any body may now calculate what the weight of the Bishop's great gun must be, that required seventy yoke of oxen to draw it. This Bishop beats Gulliver.

When men give up the use of the divine gift of reason in writing on any subject, be it religious or any thing else, there are no bounds to their extravagance, no limit to their absurdities.

The three volumes which this Bishop has written on what he calls the prophecies, contain above 1,200 pages, and he says in vol. 3, page 117, " *I have studied brevity.*" This is as marvellous as the Bishop's great gun.

flesh thereof abroad out of the house; neither shalt thou break a bone thereof."

We here see that the case as it stands in Exodus is a ceremony and not a prophecy, and totally unconnected with Jesus's bones, or any part of him.

John having thus filled up the measure of apostolic fable, concludes his book with something that beats all fable; for he says at the last verse, " And there are also many other things which Jesus did, the which if they should be written every one, I suppose that even the world itself, could not contain the books that should be written."

This is what in vulgar life is called a *thumper*; that is, not only a lie, but a lie beyond the line of possibility : besides which, it is an absurdity, for if they should be written in the world, the world would contain them.—Here ends the examination of the passages called prophecies.

I HAVE now, reader, gone through and examined all the passages which the four books of Matthew, Mark, Luke, and John, quote from the Old Testament, and call them prophecies of Jesus Christ. When I first set down to this examination, I expected to find a cause for some censure, but little did I expect to find them so utterly destitute of truth, and of all pretensions to it, as I have shewn them to be.

The practice which the writers of those books employ is not more false than it is absurd. They state some trifling case of the person they call Jesus Christ, and then cut out a sentence from some passages of the Old Testament and call it a prophecy of that case. But when the words thus cut out are restored to the place they are taken from, and read with the words before and after them, they give the lie to the New Testament. A short instance or two of this will suffice for the whole.

They make Joseph to dream of an angel, who informs him that Herod is dead, and tells him to come with the child out of Egypt. They then cut out a sentence from the book of Hosea, " Out of Egypt have I called my Son," and apply it as a prophecy in that case.

The words, " And called my Son out of Egypt," are in the Bible ;—but what of that? They are only part of a passage, and not a whole passage, and stand immediately connected with other words, which shew they refer to the children of Israel coming out of Egypt in the time of Pharoah, and to the idolatry they committed afterwards.

Again they tell us, that when the soldiers came to break

the legs of the crucified persons, they found Jesus was already dead, and therefore did not break his. They then, with some alteration of the original, cut out a sentence from Exodus, " A bone of him shall not be broken," and apply it as a prophecy of that case.

The words, " Neither shall ye break a bone thereof," (for they have altered the text) are in the Bible—but what of that? They are, as in the former case, only part of a passage, and not a whole passage, and when read with the words they are immediately joined to, shew it is the bones of a he-lamb or a he-goat of which the passage speaks.

These repeated forgeries and falsifications create a well-founded suspicion, that all the cases spoken of concerning the person called Jesus Christ are *made cases*, on purpose to lug in, and that very clumsily, some broken sentences from the Old Testament, and apply them as prophecies of those cases; and that so far from his being the Son of God, he did not exist even as a man—that he is merely an imaginary or allegorical character, as Apollo, Hercules, Jupiter, and all the deities of antiquity were. There is no history written at the time Jesus Christ is said to have lived that speaks of the existence of such a person, even as a man.

Did we find in any other book, pretending to give a system of religion, the falsehoods, falsifications, contradictions, and absurdities, which are to be met with in almost every page of the Old and New Testament, all the priests of the present day, who supposed themselves capable, would triumphantly shew their skill in criticism, and cry-it down as a most glaring imposition. But since the books in question belong to their own trade and profession, they, or at least many of them, seek to stifle every enquiry into them, and abuse those who have the honesty and the courage to do it.

When a book, as is the case with the Old and New Testament, is ushered into the world under the title of being the WORD OF GOD, it ought to be examined with the utmost strictness, in order to know if it has a well-founded claim to that title or not, and whether we are or are not imposed upon: for as no poison is so dangerous as that which poisons the physic, so no falsehood is so fatal as that which is made an article of faith.

This examination becomes more necessary, because when the New Testament was written, I might say invented, the art of printing was not known, and there were no other copies of the Old Testament than written copies. A written copy of that book would cost about as much as six hundred common printed Bibles now cost. Consequently, the book

was in the hands but of very few persons, and these chiefly
of the Church. This gave an opportunity to the writers of
the New Testament to make quotations from the Old Testament as they pleased, and call them prophecies, with very
little danger of being detected. Besides which, the terrors
and inquisitorial fury of the Church, like what they tell us
of the flaming sword that turned every way, stood sentry
over the New Testament; and time, which brings every
thing else to light, has served to thicken the darkness that
guards it from detection.

Were the New Testament now to appear for the first
time, every priest of the present day would examine it line
by line, and compare the detached sentences it calls prophecies with the whole passages in the Old Testament whence
they are taken. Why then do they not make the same
examination at this time, as they would make had the New
Testament never appeared before? If it be proper and
right to make it in one case, it is equally proper and right
to do it in the other case. Length of time can make no dif-
ference in the right to do it at any time. But instead of
doing this, they go on as their predecessors went on before
them, to tell the people there are prophecies of Jesus Christ,
when the truth is there are none.

They tell us that Jesus rose from the dead, and ascended
into heaven. It is very easy to say so; a great lie is as
easily told as a little one. But if he had done so, those
would have been the only circumstances respecting him that
would have differed from the common lot of man; and consequently the only case that would apply exclusively to
him, as prophecy, would be some passage in the Old Testament that foretold such things of him. But there is no passage in the Old Testament that speaks of a person who,
after being crucified, dead, and buried, should rise from the
dead, and ascend into heaven. Our prophecy-mongers
supply the silence the Old Testament guards upon such
things, by telling us of passages they call prophecies, and
that falsely so, about Joseph's dream, old clothes, broken
bones, and such like trifling stuff.

In writing upon this, as upon every other subject, I speak
a language full and intelligible. I deal not in hints and in-
timations. I have several reasons for this: First, that I
may be clearly understood. Secondly, that it may be seen
I am in earnest: And, Thirdly, because it is an affront to
truth to treat falsehood with complaisance.

I will close this treatise with a subject I have already
touched upon in the First Part of the *Age of Reason*.

The world has been amused with the term *revealed religion*

and the generality of priests apply this term to the books called the Old and New Testament. The Mahometans apply the same term to the Koran. There is no man that believes in revealed religion stronger than I do; but it is not the reveries of the Old and New Testament, nor of the Koran, that I dignify with that sacred title. That which is revelation to me, exists in something which no human mind can invent, no human hand can counterfeit or alter.

The *Word of God* is the *Creation* we behold; and this word of God revealeth to man all that is necessary for man to know of his Creator.

Do we want to contemplate his power? We see it in the immensity of his creation.

Do we want to contemplate his wisdom? We see it in the unchangeable order by which the incomprehensible whole is governed.

Do we want to contemplate his munificence? We see it in the abundance with which he fills the earth.

Do we want to contemplate his mercy? We see it in his not withholding that abundance, even from the unthankful.

Do we want to contemplate his will, so far as it respects man? The goodness he shews to all, is a lesson for our conduct to each other.

In fine—Do we want to know what God is? Search not the book called the Scripture, which any human hand might make, or any impostor invent; but the scripture called the Creation.

When, in the First Part of the *Age of Reason*, I called the Creation the true revelation of God to man, I did not know that any other person had expressed the same idea. But I lately met with the writings of Doctor Conyers Middleton, published the beginning of last century, in which he expresses himself in the same manner, with respect to the Creation, as I have done in the *Age of Reason*.

He was Principal Librarian of the University of Camridge, in England, which furnished him with extensive opportunities of reading, and necessarily required he should be well acquainted with the dead as well as the living languages. He was a man of a strong original mind; had the courage to think for himself, and the honesty to speak his thoughts.

He made a journey to Rome, from whence he wrote letters to shew that the forms and ceremonies of the Romish Christian Church were taken from the degenerate state of the heathen mythology, as it stood in the latter times of the Greeks and Romans. He attacked without ceremony the miracles which the Church pretended to perform; and in one of his treatises, he calls the *Creation* a *revelation*. The

priests of England of that day, in order to defend their cita-
del by first defending its out-works, attacked him for attack·
ing the Roman ceremonies; and one of them censures him
for calling the *Creation* a *revelation*—he thus replies to him:

"One of them," says he, "appears to be scandalized by
the title of *revelation*, which I have given to that discovery
which God made of himself in the visible works of his Creation.   Yet it is no other than what the wise in all ages have
given to it, who consider it as the most authentic and indisputable revelation which God has ever given of himself,
from the beginning of the world to this day.   It was this by
which the first notice of him was revealed to the inhabitants
of the earth, and by which alone it has been kept up ever
since among the several nations of it.   From this, the reason
of man was enabled to trace out his nature and attributes,
and by a gradual deduction of consequences, to learn his
own nature also, with all the duties belonging to it which
relate either to God or to his fellow-creatures.   This constitution of things was ordained by God, as a universal law
or rule of conduct to man—the source of all his knowledge
—the test of all truth, by which all subsequent revelations,
which are supposed to have been given by God in any other
manner, must be tried, and cannot be received as divine
any further than as they are found to tally and coincide
with this original standard.

"It was this divine law which I referred to in the passage
above recited, (meaning the passage on which they had attacked him) being desirous to excite the reader's attention
to it, as it would enable him to judge more freely of the argument I was handling.   For by contemplating this law, he
would discover the genuine way which God himself has
marked out to us for the acquisition of true knowledge; not
from the authority or reports of our fellow-creatures, but
from the information of the facts and material objects which
in his providential distribution of worldly things, he hath
presented to the perpetual observation of our senses.   For
as it was from these that his existence and nature, the most
important articles of all knowledge, were first discovered
to man, so that grand discovery furnished new light towards
tracing out the rest, and made all the inferior subjects of
human knowledge more easily discoverable to us by the
same method.

"I had another view likewise in the same passages, and
applicable to the same end, of giving the reader a more enlarged notion of the question in dispute, who, by turning his
thoughts to reflect on the works of the Creator, as they are
manifested to us in this fabric of the world, could not fail to

observe, that they are all of them great, noble, and suitable to the majesty of his nature, carrying with them the proofs of their origin, and shewing themselves to be the production of an all-wise and almighty Being; and by accustoming his mind to these sublime reflections, he will be prepared to determine, whether those miraculous interpositions so confidently affirmed to us by the primitive Fathers, can reasonably be thought to make a part in the grand scheme of the divine administration, or whether it be agreeable that God, who created all things by his will, and can give what turn to them he pleases by the same will, should, for the particular purposes of his government and the services of the Church, *descend to the expedient of visions and revelations*, granted sometimes to boys for the instruction of the elders, and sometimes to women to settle the fashion and length of their veils, and sometimes to pastors of the Church, to enjoin them to ordain one man a lecturer, another a priest;—or that he should scatter a profusion of miracles around the stake of a martyr, yet all of them vain and insignificant, and without any sensible effect, either of preserving the life, or of easing the sufferings of the saint; or even of mortifying his persecutors, who were always left to enjoy the full triumph of their cruelty, and the poor martyr to expire in a miserable death. When these things, I say, are brought to the original test, and compared with the genuine and indisputable works of the Creator, how minute, how trifling, how contemptible must they be?—and how incredible must it be thought, that for the instruction of his Church, God should employ ministers so precarious, unsatisfactory, and inadequate, as the ecstacies of women and boys, and the visions of interested priests, which were derided at the very time by men of sense to whom they were proposed.

" That this universal law (continues Middleton, meaning the law revealed in the works of the creation) was actually revealed to the heathen world long before the Gospel was known, we learn from all the principal sages of antiquity, who made it the capital subject of their studies and writings.

" Cicero (says Middleton) has given us a short abstract of it in a fragment still remaining from one of his books on government, which (says Middleton) I shall here transcribe in his own words, as they will illustrate my sense also, in the passages that appear, so dark and dangerous to my antagonist.

" The true law (it is Cicero that speaks) is right reason conformable to the nature of things, constant, eternal, diffused through all, which calls us to duty by commanding—

4

deters us from sin by forbidding; which never loses its in-
fluence with the good, nor ever preserves it with the wicked.
This law cannot be over-ruled by any other, nor abrogated
in whole or in part; nor can we be absolved from it either
by the senate or by the people; nor are we to seek any
other comment or interpreter of it but itself; nor can there
be one law at Rome and another at Athens—one now and
another hereafter; but the same eternal immutable law
comprehends all nations at all times, under one common
master and governor of all—God. He is the inventor, pro-
pounder, enacter of this law; and whoever will not obey it
must first renounce himself and throw off the nature of man;
by doing which, he will suffer the greatest punishments,
though he should escape all the other torments which are
commonly believed to be prepared for the wicked." Here
ends the quotation from Cicero.

"Our Doctors (continues Middleton) perhaps will look
on this as RANK DEISM; but let them call it what they will,
I shall ever avow and defend it as the fundamental, essen-
tial, and vital part of all true religion." Here ends the
quotation from Middleton.

I have here given the reader two sublime extracts from
men who lived in ages of time far remote from each other,
but who thought alike. Cicero lived before the time in
which they tell us Christ was born. Middleton may be
called a man of our own time, as he lived within the same
century with ourselves.

In Cicero we see that vast superiority of mind, that sub-
limity of right reasoning and justness of ideas which man
acquires, not by studying Bibles and Testaments, and the
theology of schools built thereon, but by studying the Creator in the immensity and unchangeable order of his creation,
and the immutability of his law. "There cannot," says
Cicero, "be one law now, and another hereafter; but the
same eternal immutable law comprehends all nations, at all
times under one common master and governer of all—God."
But according to the doctrine of schools which priests have
set up, we see one law called the *Old Testament*, given in
one age of the world, and another law, called the *New Testament*, given in another age of the world. As all this is
contradictory to the eternal immutable nature, and the
unerring and unchangeable wisdom of God, we must be
compelled to hold this doctrine to be false, and the old and
the new law, called the Old and the New Testament, to be
impositions, fables, and forgeries.

In Middleton, we see the manly eloquence of an enlarged

mind and the genuine sentiments of a true believer in his Creator. Instead of reposing his faith on books, by whatever name they may be called, whether Old Testaments or New, he fixes the creation as the great original standard by which every other thing called the word, or work of God, is to be tried. In this we have an indisputable scale whereby to measure every word or work imputed to him. If the thing so imputed carries not in itself the evidence of the same almightiness of power, of the same unerring truth and wisdom, and the same unchangeable order in all its parts, as are visibly demonstrated to our senses, and comprehensible by our reason, in the magnificent fabric of the universe, that word or that work is not of God. Let then the two books called the Old and New Testament be tried by this rule, and the result will be, that the authors of them, whoever they were, will be convicted of forgery.

The invariable principles, and unchangeable order, which regulate the movements of all the parts that compose the universe, demonstrate both to our senses and our reason that its creator is a God of unerring truth. But the Old Testament, besides the numberless, absurd, and bagatelle stories it tells of God, represents him as a God of deceit, a God not to be confided in. Ezekiel makes God to say, chap. 14. ver. 9, "And if the prophet be deceived when he hath spoken a thing, I, *the Lord, have deceived that prophet.*" And at the 20th chap. ver. 25, he makes God, in speaking of the children of Israel to say, " *Wherefore I gave them statutes that were not good, and judgments by which they could not live.*" This, so far from being the word of God, is horrid blasphemy against him. Reader, put thy confidence in thy God, and put no trust in the Bible.

The same Old Testament, after telling us that God created the heavens and the earth in six days, makes the same almighty power and eternal wisdom employ itself in giving directions how a priest's garments should be cut, and what sort of stuff they should be made of, and what their offerings should be, gold, and silver, and brass, and blue, and purple, and scarlet, and fine linen, and goats' hair, and rams' skins dyed red, and badgers' skins, &c. chap. XXV. ver. 3; and in one of the pretended prophecies I have just examined, God is made to give directions how they should kill, cook, and eat a he-lamb or a he-goat. And Ezekiel, chap. iv. to fill up the measure of abominable absurdity, makes God to order him to take " *wheat, and barley, and beans, and lentiles, and millet, and fitches, and make a loaf or a cake thereof, and bake it with human dung and*

eat it ;" but as Ezekiel complained that this mess was too
strong for his stomach, the matter was compromised from
man's to cow dung, Ezekiel, chap. iv. Compare all this
ribaldry, blasphemously called the word of God, with the
almighty power that created the universe, and whose eternal wisdom directs and governs all its mighty movements,
and we shall be at a loss to find a name sufficiently contemptible for it.

In the promises which the Old Testament pretends that
God made to his people, the same derogatory ideas of him
prevail. It makes God to promise to Abraham, that his
seed should be like the stars in heaven and the sand on the
sea-shore for multitude, and that he would give them the
land of Canaan as their inheritance for ever. But observe,
reader, how the preformance of this promise was to begin,
and then ask thy own reason, if the wisdom of God, whose
power is equal to his will, could consistently with that power
and that wisdom, make such a promise.

The performance of the promise was to begin, according
to that book, by four hundred years of bondage and affliction. Genesis, chap. xv. ver. 13, *" And God said unto
Abraham, know of a surety, that thy seed shall be a stranger in a land that is not theirs, and shall serve them, and
they shall afflict them four hundred years."* This promise
then to Abraham, and his seed for ever, to inherit the land
of Canaan, had it been a fact instead of a fable, was to
operate, in the commencement of it, as a curse upon all the
people and their children, and their children's children for
four hundred years.

But the case is, the book of Genesis was written after the
bondage in Egypt had taken place ; and in order to get rid
of the disgrace of the Lord's chosen people, as they called
themselves, being in bondage to the Gentiles, they make
God to be the author of it, and annex it as a condition to
a pretended promise ; as if God, in making that promise,
had exceeded his power in performing it, and consequently
his wisdom in making it, and was obliged to compromise
with them for one half, and with the Egyptians, to whom
they were to be in bondage, for the other half.

Without degrading my own reason by bringing those
wretched and contemptible tales into a comparative view,
with the almighty power and eternal wisdom, which the
Creator hath demonstrated to our senses in the creation of
the universe, I will confine myself to say, that if we compare them with the divine and forcible sentiments of Cicero,
the result will be, that the human mind has degenerated by

believing them. Man, in a state of grovelling superstition, from which he has not courage to rise, looses the energy of his mental powers.

I will not tire the reader with more observations on the Old Testament.

As to the New Testament, if it be brought and tried by that standard, which, as Middleton wisely says, God has revealed to our senses, of his almighty power and wisdom in the creation and government of the visible universe, it will be found equally as false, paltry, and absurd, as the Old.

Without entering, in this place, into any other argument, that the story of Christ is of human invention and not of divine origin, I will confine myself to shew that it is derogatory to God, by contrivance of it; because the means it supposes God to use, are not adequate to the end to be obtained; and therefore are derogatory to the almightness of his power, and the eternity of his wisdom.

The New Testament supposes that God sent his Son upon earth to make a new covenant with man; which the Church calls *the covenant of Grace*, and to instruct mankind in a new doctrine, which it calls *Faith*, meaning thereby, not faith in God, for Cicero and all true Deists always had and always will have this; but faith in the person called Jesus Christ, and that whoever had not this faith should, to use the words of the New Testament, be DAMNED.

Now if this were a fact, it is consistent with that attribute of God, called his Goodness, that no time should be lost in letting poor unfortunate man know it; and as that goodness was united to the almighty power, and that power to almighty wisdom, all the means existed in the hand of the Creator to make it known immediately over the whole earth, in a manner suitable to the almightiness of his divine nature, and with evidence that would not leave man in doubt; for it is always incumbent upon us, in all cases, to believe that the Almighty always acts, not by imperfect means as imperfect man acts, but consistently with his almightiness. It is this only that can become the infallible criterion by which we can possibly distinguish the works of God from the works of man.

Observe now, reader, how the comparison between this supposed mission of Christ, on the belief or disbelief of which they say man was to be saved or damned—observe, I say, how the comparison between this and the almighty power and wisdom of God, demonstrated to our senses in the visible creation, goes on.

The Old Testament tells us that God created the heavens and the earth, and every thing therein, in six days. The term *six days* is ridiculous enough when applied to God; but leaving out that absurdity, it contains the idea of almighty power acting unitedly with almighty wisdom, to produce an immense work, that of the creation of the universe and every thing therein, in a short time.

Now as the eternal salvation of man is of much greater importance than his creation, and as that salvation depends, as the New Testament tells us, on man's knowledge of and belief in the person of Jesus Christ, it necessarily follows from our belief in the goodness and justice of God, and our knowledge of his almighty power and wisdom, as demonstrated in the creation, that ALL THIS, if true, would be made known to all parts of the world, in as little time, at least, as was employed in making the world. To suppose the Almighty would pay greater regard and attention to the creation and organization of inanimate matter, than he would to the salvation of innumerable millions of souls, which himself had created, " as the image of himself," is to offer an insult to his goodness and his justice.

Now observe, reader, how the promulgation of this pretended salvation by a knowledge of, and a belief in Jesus Christ, went on, compared with the work of creation.

In the first place, it took longer time to make the child than to make the world, for nine months were passed away and totally lost in a state of pregnancy; which is more than forty times longer time than God employed in making the world, according to the Bible account. Secondly—several years of Christ's life were lost in a state of human infancy. But the universe was in maturity the moment it existed. Thirdly—Christ, as Luke asserts, was thirty years old before he began to preach what they call his mission. Millions of souls died in the mean time without knowing it. Fourthly— it was above three hundred years from that time before the book called the New Testament was compiled into a written copy, before which time there was no such book. Fifthly— it was above a thousand years after that, before it could be circulated; because neither Jesus nor his apostles had knowledge of, or were inspired with the art of printing; and consequently, as the means for making it universally known did not exist, the means were not equal to the end, and therefore it is not the work of God.

I will here subjoin the nineteenth Psalm, which is truly Deistical, to shew how universally and instantaneously the works of God make themselves known, compared with this pretended salvation by Jesus Christ.

Psalm 19th. "The heavens declare the glory of God, and the firmament sheweth his handy-work—Day unto day uttereth speech, and night unto night sheweth knowledge—There is no speech nor language where their voice is not heard—Their line is gone out through all the earth, and their words to the end of the world. In them hath he set a chamber for the Sun. Which is as a bridegroom coming out of his chamber, and rejoiceth as a strong man to run a race—his going forth is from the end of the heaven, and his circuit unto the ends of it, and there is nothing hid from the heat thereof."

Now, had the news of salvation by Jesus Christ been inscribed on the face of the Sun and the Moon, in characters that all nations would have understood, the whole earth had known it in twenty-four hours, and all nations would have believed it; whereas, though it is now almost two thousand years since, as they tell us, Christ came upon earth, not a twentieth part of the people of the earth know any thing of it, and among those who do, the wiser part do not believe it.

I have now, reader, gone through all the passages called prophecies of Jesus Christ, and shewn there is no such thing.

I have examined the story told of Jesus Christ, and compared the several circumstances of it with that revelation, which, as Middleton wisely says, God has made to us of his power and wisdom in the structure of the universe, and by which every thing ascribed to him is to be tried. The result is, that the story of Christ has not one trait, either in its character, or in the means employed, that bears the least resemblance to the power and wisdom of God, as demonstrated in the creation of the universe. All the means are human means, slow, uncertain, and inadequate to the accompl is ment of the end proposed, and therefore the whole is a fabulous invention, and undeserving of credit.

The priests of the present day profess to believe it. They gain their living by it, and they exclaim against something they call infidelity. I will define what it is. HE THAT BELIEVES IN THE STORY OF CHRIST IS AN INFIDEL TO GOD.

THOMAS PAINE.

APPENDIX.

CONTRADICTORY DOCTRINES

IN THE NEW TESTAMENT,

BETWEEN

Matthew and Mark.

In the New Testament, Mark, chap. xvi. ver. 16. it is said, " He that believeth and is baptized shall be saved ; he that believeth not shall be damned." This is making salvation, or in other words, the happiness of man after this life, to depend entirely on believing, or on what the Christians call faith.

But the 25th chapter of *The Gospel according to Matthew* makes Jesus Christ to preach a direct contrary doctrine to " The Gospel according to Mark ;" for it makes salvation, or the future happiness of man, to depend entirely on *good works ;* and those good works are not works done to God, for he needs them not, but good works done to man.

The passage referred to in Matthew is the account there given of what is called the last day, or the day of judgment, where the whole world is represented to be divided into two parts, the righteous and the unrighteous, metaphorically called the *sheep* and the *goats.*

To the one part, called the righteous, or the sheep, it says, " Come ye blessed of my Father, inherit the kingdom prepared for you from the beginning of the world—for I was an hungered and ye gave me meat—I was thirsty and ye gave me drink—I was a stranger and ye took me in—Naked and ye clothed me—I was sick and ye visited me—I was in prison and ye came unto me."

Printed in the USA
CPSIA information can be obtained
at www.ICGtesting.com
LVHW021617061023
760371LV00005B/77